THIS WALKER BOOK BELONGS TO:

For Billie
S.G.

For Les and Nell
C.S.

First published 1987 by Walker Books Ltd
87 Vauxhall Walk, London SE11 5HJ

This edition published 1988
Reprinted 1989, 1991, 1993

Text © 1987 Sally Grindley
Illustrations © 1987 Clive Scruton

Printed in Hong Kong by
Sheck Wah Tong Printing Press Ltd

British Library Cataloguing in Publication Data
A catalogue record for this book is
available from the British Library.
ISBN 0-7445-1064-3

FOUR BLACK PUPPIES

written by Sally Grindley
illustrated by Clive Scruton

WALKER BOOKS
LONDON

Four black puppies in a basket,

fast asleep.

One black puppy waking up.

One black puppy

going for a walk.

One black puppy

pulling at an apron.

One shopping basket

falling down.

Three black puppies running

in to have a look.

Three black puppies see...

A GHOST!

One white puppy

chasing three black puppies.

four puppies running

round and round.

All four puppies

running back to bed.

All four puppies in a basket,

fast asleep.

MORE WALKER PAPERBACKS
For You to Enjoy

CAT AND DOG
by David Lloyd/Clive Scruton

A bold and breathless chase that invites plenty of participation from young children.

ISBN 0-7445-1317-0   £3.99

SIDNEY THE MONSTER
by David Wood/Clive Scruton

Winner of the Acorn Award.

Sidney the monster frightens everyone – except young Millie, who thinks he's hilarious!

"Great fun… Incredibly silly illustrations guarantee giggles all round."
Valerie Bierman, The Scotsman

ISBN 0-7445-1369-3   £3.99

WILLOUGHBY WALLABY
by Jez Alborough

When Willoughby Wallaby comes to a stop,
His friends try to give him back his hop!

"A rollicking rhyming text and outrageously funny, story-telling pictures."
Jill Bennett, British Book News

ISBN 0-7445-1484-3   £2.99

**Walker Paperbacks are available from most booksellers, or by post from
Walker Books Ltd, PO Box 11, Falmouth, Cornwall TR10 9EN.**

To order, send: Title, author, ISBN number and price for each book ordered, your full name and address, cheque or postal order
for the total amount, plus postage and packing: UK and BFPO Customers – £1.00 for first book, plus 50p for the second book
and plus 30p for each additional book to a maximum charge of £3.00. Overseas and Eire Customers – £2.00 for first book,
plus £1.00 for the second book and plus 50p per copy for each additional book.